Fast Fat Girls
In Pink Hot Pants

D1557804

Fast Fat Girls
In Pink Hot Pants

poems

Artress Bethany White

Aldabra Press

Library of Congress Control Number: 2012943199

Publisher's Cataloging-In-Publication Data
White, Artress Bethany.
   Fast fat girls in pink hot pants / Artress Bethany White.
   p. cm.
   ISBN: 978-0-9858133-0-7
   1. African Americans — Poetry. 2. Race — Poetry.
3. Women — United States — Poetry. 4. South (U.S.) — Poetry.
5. American poetry — 21st century. 6. Poetry — Women authors.
I. Title.
PS3623.H5695 F37 2012
811/.6   2012943199

The author acknowledges the following publications which first published early versions of select poems from this collection:

"Of Rattlesnakes and Beer on Sunday Morning" and "Geneva Could Have Walked to Switzerland" *Harvard Review*; "Bone and Socket" *A Tapestry of Voices: An East Tennessee Anthology*; "A Gathering of Blooms" *MELUS*: Special Issue Multi-Ethnic Poetics; "Planting Seeds" *Appalachian Journal*: Special Issue on Women in Appalachia; "Fast Fat Girls in Pink Hot Pants," "Black Snake Skin Boots," and "Etymology of a Nickname" *Black Renaissance Noire*.

Special thanks to members of the Dark Room Collective, Quincy Troupe, and Arthur White, my dad and first critic... and the many others who have encouraged me over the years.

for
Frances

CONTENTS

NORTH

New England Rebel
for Arthur L. White

I wanted you to have been
a Black Panther
when I understood
that you were a child of the 60s.
I mean, a battle was certainly brewing in you
when you left the South for the North,
unwilling to haul phosphate on a train.
Left and never looked back
on Polk County, Florida,
which we'd later learn
was the chosen region of Zora Neale Hurston's
fade into obscurity,
because the place
had that effect on people,
making them
fade away.

But no black leather,
guns, exile, and lunch counters for you;
instead, you patiently explained
that revolutionary acts
could be carried out in many ways,
yours to break the color line at the local country club
and make a million
before P. Diddy and Kanye
made it look so easy.
Oh, and sporting a Benz
when black folks from the South
still pronounced Massachusetts "Massa two sets"
and Mercedes "Mer ca deez"

Meeting James Baldwin

He was sitting in the airport all nonchalant.
At first glance, you were just
trying to catch his eye, render the black man nod
but then you took in the full face and felt
the impact of that visage and those eyes
his stepfather had despised
negating black was beautiful.

He was royalty in your eyes.
His latest, *If Beale Street Could Talk*
gracing your bookshelf
only two or three months old.
You wished you had it in your pocket,
nothing less than an autograph would do
to memorialize this moment in history.

Instead, you let the nod suffice
played it cool, knowing you knew
and he knew
what it is.

Snapshot at Prospect Terrace, Providence, RI

How amazing is this,
you looking like a dark brown version of Huey Newton.
That signature afro cut just so, and those shades
looking like cool breeze.

I know I must have thought you were the bomb
standing there holding your hand
in my pink parka.
And there was Arthur in his baby carriage,
not yet aware of family politics
and the role he would play
in this real-life drama.

There is no picture of us
the day we rode in your
new MG, the first of a series
of sporty compacts
that would eventually stop
at the Porsche 928.
We paused for ice cream
to commemorate the
little piece of Britain
you now owned.
I ordered pistachio
thinking it was lime sherbet
and with disgust
let the ball of cream roll
down the cone onto your new car.
When you erupted about the mess,
I blamed it on Arthur,
the baby, knowing that he
was too young to garner
a spanking, my nonchalant fib
an easy evasion to discipline.

The irony was
that it would not be
too many years later
when that same
innocent babe, now grown,
would total your Porsche
on a small-town highway,
careless of what money could
and couldn't buy,
like the sweet family
portrait of us standing in
the park, one copy
pulled out at holidays
like love.

Prayer Closet

I wash the evidence of their menses
from underpants and sheets
and can count on one hand the blessings
it has garnered me, this New England family that
calls me maid, as if I was born
to serve, not black like them with an American dream.

In Venezuela I used to think the white men there
were the heaviest burden I would ever have to bear,
their racist snipes
pelting my back like stones
as I hurried along the street
trying to outrun the realities of immigration.

The day finally came
when I knew I'd had enough,
took off my shoe in the street,
this *negra* that they hated so, and placed
my finger on the white sole devoid of the black
that colored the rest of my body.
Este es tu color I shouted, *este es tu color*,
this is your color
the words bitten off in my perfect Spanish.
I then placed my foot
on the street to let my latest verbal attacker know
where his color stood in relation to me.
His mouth dropped open
and I wished for a fly to gain an opportunity
as I spun on my heel and limped away.

I hide myself in the scriptures to avoid both hurts,
the old and the new.
In my Book, my persecutors
are Pharaoh's children, and I know
they will not escape the plagues.
Moses is my idol, a rescuer with God's plan,
despite the belief in a promised land
he would not live to see.

I know that you're supposed to pray
for your enemies, but after the tears,
the fasting, and the silent cries, I still
see the burning coals as my recompense.

This family I serve now eats at the resolve
of that day on a Venezuelan street.
I speak four languages: English, Spanish, the word of God,
and the one I don't talk about.
They say that you dream
in the language you know best.
By day, I sneak into my prayer closet
to talk to God
and make peace with the work I do,
at night I sleep too soundly to hear His answers.

Dragging Angela Through the Streets

I had to drag Angela through
the streets to make history real
for my English 100 students
in East New York.

Their daily battle
consisted of tripping over
crackheads to get to work
and praying for suburbs that weren't so
far away that mama could still baby-sit.

We love you teacher they claimed
as I pored over their grammatical imperfections
trying to teach them English before I could
teach them grammar.

But we were on the same page
when I brought in that 16mm tin can
holding Angela Davis's story in black and white.
I swear someone started chanting I'm black
and I'm proud as I threaded the projector.

The lights went down and we all stepped
back in time, until Emilio broke
that rapt silence with
Yo man, she's smokin' a pipe!

African for a Day
For Ngugi

What if a group of black-clad men
with machine guns
burst into this room right now?
What would you do?

The question hung in midair undisturbed,
poised expectantly, head cocked
as the students considered you
wearing deer in headlight expressions
that had no place in a university classroom.
Perhaps your tale of composing,
writing on toilet paper while imprisoned
had left them gasping like fish out of water,
interrupted their dreams
of making Wall Street salaries
from degrees in the humanities.
Here you were rhapsodizing Gikuyu,
illuming eager minds
and they were too polite to ask
how you wiped your behind in prison
if all the toilet paper went toward writing.
A classroom full of suburban white kids
save one imagining she understood
the language you spoke,
even though the closest I had
come to oppression was
being called the n-word regularly
growing up in a small Western Massachusetts town.
Still, I mimicked the sneer on your face
waiting for them to answer
that one question
sure of only one thing,
I would do what those men asked
already beginning to write my survival story in my mind
until I could secure some paper
to make it last.

Boston Meets Brooklyn

Head wrap towering a full 15 inches in the air
neck stretched long to carry the weight
of dreads, fabric, and my right
to survive another night in Bed-Sty
I walked the gauntlet of drug dealers
from subway to my front door,
just living shabby chic
because the bills were cheap.
Being taken for a Muslim regularly,
as salaam alaikums falling around my ears
making me think about prayer
and holy things,
not smoking a blunt with Biggie Smalls
and the type of girls that used to pull
my ponytails for being cute in elementary school.
Contact high from the smoke alone
made me lower my guard enough
to forget gangsters, wannabes,
Fanon, Gramsci
and the twenty-five page paper
I had yet to write,
never thinking this would be the last time
I'd hear Christopher Wallace's voice
talking late into the night
about what life would be like
when he made it Big
and everyone knew his name.

Ice Cream for Breakfast in Bed-Sty

Purists might disagree,
but the genesis of motherhood
is as humble as an erection
brushing a woman's hip bone
in that odd moment when a lover
feels like a stranger,
as you drop your eyes shyly
before his sexual nature
a mask pulled on just for you.

More difficult to remember
is the exact moment
when the crack pipe
began to compete for your attention
over a bulging belly.
Romance forgotten, he now
reminds you to think of the child
as he robs you of your hits
one after another.

Somehow your mother is the one
who keeps you from selling the first little girl
on the streets, her cherub cheeks
destined for greater things than
being whisked off by some stranger
to greener pastures for a few bucks.

Two years later, she is joined
by a sister. Everyone thinks
that it's easy to be mother and
grandmother to crack babies,
but Social Security doesn't prepare
you for everything, like watching
your grandchildren eat ice cream
for breakfast on the steps
of your brownstone
as if it's summer in March.

When Absolute Comfort
is Enough Absolution for One Day

Her gaze dropped to his parchment dry white hand
tenderly clasping her own brown one upon the tabletop.
Today he was reminded again of the importance of his calling
in spiritu et veritate, in spirit and truth,
in the person of a young black woman
eight months pregnant, no ring on her finger.

He recalled the esteemed history of the gem
of this diocese, New York's St. Patrick's Cathedral,
whose lofty halls had witnessed
so many opulent weddings.
Unprepared for God's demand to humble himself,
he made confession before her,
bypassed the "Forgive me father, for I have sinned"
and cut to the chase.
My sister had a child out of wedlock,
as if this simple statement settled the matter.
Did you know that good Catholic girls can fall, too?

She realized then who she was talking to.
This man had likely not lain
between a woman's thighs since taking his vows.
The miracle birth was his own journey
in spiritus domini, in the spirit of the Lord.
In his eyes, she, a black Madonna who deserved
the reverent prayers of the righteous.
He had learned his lessons well, accepted
that every child from any woman's womb
was a potential convert, a lamb, a disciple,
and a testimony.

Later, she often wondered what became of this priest
too polite to wipe her fallen tears
from the back of his hand, no doubt thinking
that there should be an alabaster box on call
when one needed it, but today

his hand alone would serve.
Face to face, she thought that she might
recognize him by his eyes, kind and tender.
If so, it would be enough to tell him
that, *del gratia,* by the grace of God
she had survived to love again
and could now toast him with the words
Domino optimo maximo,
to the Lord, the best and greatest.

Talking Tennessee

The New England winter I played
Dolly Parton's single "Me and Little Andy"
over and over on my Close 'N Play
I was nowhere near the Smokies,
knew nothing of country music,
or what made me work that tune
until I could mimic pathos with a Tennessee twang
like I understood real poverty
and knew why a child and her puppy
going to Jesus for Christmas
could win my heart.

SOUTH

A Lady's Carriage
(On hearing a horse and carriage make the wedding circuit
around Triangle Park, Lexington, KY)

Summer Saturday morning and I wake start to the clip clop
of a horse's hooves under my window.
Unwinding from bed to drink in a weak summer breeze,
I cup my breasts along one forearm and pull the shade aside
to see newlyweds in carriaged splendor,
before turning again in disgust
to witness my own rumpled and empty altar.

Marriage is a mystery that begins in the mind with rein and bit
placed and held by a husband's hand, a command to yield.
Like Moses's warning to the Israelites to shave
the head of any captive woman
they desired to marry, an unseen hand guides
the scissors across my scalp until I am bald,
new again in this city
that has held me captive too long.

It is synesthesia that makes me jump
at movement, sudden sound.
I sit nervously in a movie house
and wonder if this timidity
will follow me to the marriage bed.
Blinking stars above me in the retro ceiling
of the Kentucky Theater remind me
of the first time.
Memory like a mischievous voice whispers and I shiver
as I did at the hands of a Haitian lover
a good Catholic boy who asked me if I was pure,
trying to be sure too late.

At night I beg to know the finish.
How many months of instruction does my man need
before he is certain I will surrender,
will do all that I can to please,
be remade, complete, for his hands only?

Honor thy mother and thy father
that thou days may be long
and I say wait for your husband,
wait for your lover.

Planting Seeds

The place of conception, the sowing
should have meant she was freeborn
in this city of brotherly love,
where once declarations were signed
that ignored those black sons of some other God.
What monumental things can take
place when two poets collide?
Northern-born affirmative action babes
affirming that generations are
the stuff of guttural cries and
lingering embraces. Life like
the spark of inspiration,
pen to the page.

Reverse migration is not like reentering the womb
as a seedling but has more to do with history
like a tender echo grasping at the horizon
looking for a good place to stop, a turning back
to look for answers to questions of why me,
why you and now she.

Seeds often land on conflicted ground.
Tennessee and Kentucky
slave states that claimed
to spawn hospitality in this new South.
The rituals so specific they should have
been written down.
Never go to someone's house invited
with empty hands like a barbarian
with no code to follow.
Don't even think about sounding off
on your neighbor in a large group.
Someone will suddenly claim kin
and you may not leave the building alive,
victim of hillbilly justice over a second cousin
nobody in the family liked anyway
but blood is blood so…

In the middle of new ground
our child, a wild thing
that toyed with the idea
of walking barefoot
as if it were her birthright,
not understanding
that Southern caste thing
that could brand you for life
though nobody ever used the term black trash,
but there she was
toes skimming dew
trying to establish some new lexicon.

Who is this child of noble birth,
symbol of the mingling
of blood across regional lines
amalgamation that threatened
genealogical order?
This tongue she spoke, so alien
its attributes a testament to her
identification with some other clan.
Cuss instead of *curse*,
Sutheren stated as a three-syllable word
instead of *Southern* with a distinct two-syllable snap.
Was this what living in Appalachia could
do to a family? Change the order of genes
like transplanted seeds
birthing a rebel child.

Surely the Civil War Was Not Begun
Over a Plate of Grits

The story would go something like this,
I was sitting in a friend's kitchen
as she labored over a pot, wooden spoon in hand
when she asked if I had ever eaten cheese grits.
My being black and from New England
must have confused her.
My immediate impulse was to pose
several questions of my own—
but her smile was brighter than the afternoon sunlight
slanting across her Julia Childs butcher board table,
too bright to crush.
Admittedly, sometimes a simple yes
is the best policy.
Yes.

Children are able to cross the color line
so much easier than adults.
Had it not occurred to her that
more than people had moved
during the Great Migration.
The South had traveled
over the Mason-Dixon line
and into northern kitchens, too.
I had never pondered the complexity of a grit
or confused them with Cream of Wheat.
Yet here I was in a kitchen trying to forget
history and race in the South,
to imagine that my friend's husband
was not closet Klan,
to believe that the existence
of their rich Northern relatives
somehow meant that their Southern kin
hadn't lynched people,
to believe that our children

would still like each other in high school
and maybe even consider dating
without their sweet little blond boy
ever calling my daughter the "n" word.

The grits are done and I pray that they are not lumpy
or I will light into this woman
with the same quiet vehemence
of my sanctified grandmother
when the weight of history
became too much for her to bear.

Black Snake Skin Boots

There is a certain smile that graces the face
of white men when they see
an attractive black woman
that recalls images of white uniforms
slamming pots and wandering hands
over the behinds of resistant black maids.

I'd encountered it last in White, Georgia
maybe once a sundown town,
or with a name like that, a place
that black folks should never visit,
even at high noon. But, boots in hand
I braved the stigma of nomenclature.

As soon as I entered
this backwoods cobbler, I felt the compulsion
to back out slowly.
At the sudden *Howdy gal*,
a bead of sweat began a downward
slide along my spine
to the tune of Dixie.

What had convinced me
that snake skin cowboy boots
would suddenly make me belong?
Here, I understood I was in a new nation.
The Confederate flag tacked
proudly against that backroom wall
did not attest to my nativity.

But my prized possessions
needed work.
I would have given anything
to be back on the Lower East Side

where I had purchased these Texan beauties,
where East met West without the shackles of history,
where only four blocks further west
I could have them re-heeled
by the best Italian shoemakers,
back in a city where multiculturalism
made sense instead of in White
where black and white
was as complex and simple
as telling this man with naked lust in his eyes
not to get off calling me gal.

"I shoved him in a closet set
Against the wall. This would but let
Him breathe two minutes more, or three,
Before they dragged him out to be
Queer fruit upon some outraged tree"
from Countee Cullen's "The Black Christ"

Dying By the Rood

I can only wonder what it was like
a man, a tree, and history.
After fear comes a determined resignation.
Just ask anyone who has given birth,
said goodbye to a lover too soon,
finally accepted the creep of old age,
or seen life flash before them
in a heart-stopping moment.

I can only imagine that final stretch
pale palm raised to ask for help,
praying that God would call out one
among these white faces
to raise his voice and say
Naw boys, y'all go on home now,
we're not going to do this tonight.
And you would accept the apology,
allow the rope to slip over your head
and drop from your wrists,
head home for supper like nothing had
ever happened, wiping the blood from
your shattered face with a grateful sleeve.

Instead, the slow creep of grim acceptance
that your name was not Isaac
and there would be no ram
in the bush to make
this executioner's noose pass over you.

With no voice left, your mind alone screams
that you'd never even looked
at that white woman.
Would never
touch another woman period
if you could only walk away.

Still, something compels you to look up.
Maybe if your eyes could only reach heaven
that man after the order of Melchizedek
would hear your prayer
and release this last breath stuck
in your lungs, keep your bound knuckles
from scraping this tree.

Hiding the Truth
for Arthur De Gobineau[1]

This moment in history is my chance
to have my say.
It is brilliant to hate blacks,
Mongols.
When I write about the cultural
habits of the latter, I sometimes wonder
how it would feel
to touch their glossy black hair like
corn silk without kink or curl.
Under my fingertips this secret joy
to know what I could have been.

No drop of blood to carry weight
in my hair and features, undetected
like the threat
my cousin whispered
when I was still a boy and quick to anger.
Imagine, he said, *if your maman was black,*
the words like a curse whispered
into my ear, a taunt that made me wonder
about the origins of man.

A French woman, my mother
so delicately boned
she could never harbor
the taint of the enemy
whose story I tell
because it is my right,
not a clever ploy
to hide my own racial doubt.

[1] Arthur De Gobineau was a nineteenth-century race theorist whose racist
perspectives have influenced generations.

Memory and Apocrypha
In memory of Dan White

Memory, a testament of a life
a text verifiable by photographs,
eyewitness account, consensus.

He was
hands
rough and stiff
that hurt to bend,
would crack if tried.
Hands no lotion
could soften.

His knees
better than a chair,
a grandfather's knee like a throne:
A place to sit and hear
the latest gossip
slide unchecked
from adult lips.

His money
back when a nickel
could actually buy
delivered like a fortune into my hand.

In the gaps of my recollection
apocrypha
those books that tell a story
outside the primary content.
A face, the exact features of which
memory could not recall.

How simple or complex his thoughts
no four-year old could know,
only the intrusion of memory again
as they lowered him into the ground
and said he was going
where I could not follow.

Memory, a set of images
and apocrypha
the recollections
of others,
where consensus can't be reached.

Pennies Come Payday
for Evelena Hayes

Before Walmart there was the company store
that place where your boss took the rest
of your life so that you belonged to him 100%.
Sold everything from crackers to kerosene
to the overalls for your first day of work
that it took you darn near three months to pay for.

There was a price for living rent free.
Company homes shooting distance
from the mine where you labored
like a modern-day slave quarters.
It took God to keep
you from spitting in that boss's eye
as he looked at your paycheck
then into your face
Gotta big one this week.
You swallowing quick to chuckle that fake
good-natured laugh that showed you
held no rancor for phosphate mines and high-priced
dry goods you were forced to buy on credit.

Sometimes your biggest dream was to
have enough left in a check to buy
each of your children a couple of
pieces of candy just to see their
faces split by smiles,
their cries of *Thank you daddy* raining
around your ears
a fit measure of your manhood.

Etymology of a Nickname

It came down to two possibilities,
the first, a diminutive of the word newt
the peninsula variety common
to the Florida panhandle,
an amphibious creature
beginning life as a tadpole,
sprouting appendages as an adult.

After all,
they said it was my grandfather
who had named me,
possibly saw me as a human tadpole
at nine months language undeveloped,
a larvae, unable to walk unassisted
semi-terrestrial,
still more adaptable to water
than land,
and able to hold my breath
when submerged
naturally.

But no one knew
for sure.
The second possibility,
an utterance that surprised even my grandfather
one day when he was trying to shout
to keep me from crawling
into mischief,
the syllables of my name
refusing to come quickly enough
so God sent a replacement
that sounded like newt-chi
and I stopped mid-crawl
at the novelty of the word,
looked over my shoulder
with a toothless grin.
Proud of his ingenuity

he informed everyone that
this was my nickname
and it stuck.
It was years later
when I learned the truth,
that I was actually the recipient
of an evolved
version of Mussolini's nickname
"Il Duce," the leader,
adapted by my own
father, inspired by the dictatorial
qualities I exhibited as a child
demanding attention.
He softened the words
to peacekeeping Italian, *DaNuci*,
the language like a new toy
on his tongue.
It was he who made sure
this appellation migrated from
New England to Florida,
my grandfather forced to translate Italian
into southern speak.

No linguist, merely a scribe
I now know the contentment that comes
from seeing another family mystery solved.

Of the Order *Coleoptera*

The scarab beetle
its back as black
and shiny as
patent leather shoes
on Easter Sunday morning
lobster-like claws
so inviting under a
magnifying glass,
inspired evil
deeds in the most
innocent of boyhood minds.

The Lakeland Ledger might
have reported a decline
in this local species
of beetle
due to climate change
or the result
of a fowl suddenly finding
it had to adjust its palette
or starve in this 21st century
environmental mayhem.

What the paper would not report,
the number of times
I had been threatened
as a child
by cousins who knew
how much beetle claws
loved the soft wool
of braids come undone.
A love so dear
that the sweet sound
of terrified girl screams
could be heard
from two blocks away
and were well worth
the switching sure to follow.

Geneva Could Have Walked to Switzerland

The third time she tried to leave the porch that morning
they put me in charge. My job was to let any adult
in shouting distance know that my grandmother's sister,
Geneva, was attempting once again to walk out the door
to parts unknown.
I knew her as Devil, a nickname that began as expletive
and finally ended in laughter and love.
A neighbor would often remark
She almost got away from you, didn't she?
As I tugged her by the hand back from the roadside.
Still embarrassed about being put in control of an adult
at age five, I merely smiled ascent and whispered
Come on Devil under my breath.

Unlike other elderly family,
who faded and finally succumbed
to the reaper's call, I could not remember her passing.
My investigation into her sudden absence
always met with the same whimsical laugh
and question: *You remember her?*
For memorable she was.
The only woman in our family not of that telltale pecan color
minus the veins of black running through it.
Though some might start out walnut,
the penetrating Florida sun had a way of making all
shades of black equal in the long run.
Not so Geneva, she was the color
of vanilla ice cream with sweet caramel swirled into it.
When she and my granny stood together,
the only way to tell they were sisters
was by word of mouth.

No one talked about Alzheimer's then,
Geneva was just hardheaded and wouldn't stay put.
I still feel this compulsion to find her grave,
to make sure they got the name right and had not
chiseled Devil somewhere on her tombstone,
another rascal who liked to roam the earth.

Royce's Funeral Home

More intriguing than white shoes in winter,
a mourner's prayer itches under his skin.
Church fan deliveryman-cum-undertaker
he was more watcher than participant.
Sweaty faces coming down from religious ecstasy
would read all about his business.
He took pride in the fact
that for bored children in Sunday pews,
his advertising was a first primer
on the road to literacy — funeral a
three syllable word that everyone whispered.

When the jumping and praising stopped,
he was there, Johnny on the spot.
They didn't walk into his office,
and they certainly didn't walk out.

He imagined the body rituals as a sort of ceremony
like marriage, as he gently draped a sheet over a lady's hips,
whispering *no sex where you're going*
into her frozen ear.
One-time choir boy reaching out to persuade,
working his fingers around her stiff hand
like a date she didn't want.

This creator shakes his head
at rigor mortis
the kind of truth
nobody wants to write a song about,
that place in the hymn where you
start to hum, like the old people say,
so the devil won't steal the words, like breath,
right out your mouth.

Fast Fat Girls In Pink Hot Pants

Summers in Immokalee, Florida
were a lesson in multiculturalism and economics.
As kids, we were told to avoid
the Mexicans because they were migrants,
seasonal workers with little chance of social mobility
and even less English.
I would long to try the depth
of my elementary Spanish on them, but would
become suddenly shy after the initial *Hola!*

But our designated playmate was a heavyset black girl
with unwashed hair,
whom my grandmother
insisted we be nice to
because she'd had no advantages.
I begged to differ.
Her size gave her the advantage to be a bully,
and her sweat, unwashed for days,
was enough to make the eyes water and the knees weak.

My immediate dislike of this playmate
five years ahead of both my sister and I
was her disregard for truth.
She once asked to see my China.
Unfamiliar with the turn of phrase,
I literally believed she was making
reference to the country in Asia
and asked her to get a map
and I'd show her.
She frowned in consternation,
looked at me like I was ignorant,
and pointed to her shorts below the waist.
Ten, but no fool, I realized
that she was
making reference to my vagina,
leaving off the letters "v" and "a" and
pronouncing the "g" as "c."

I turned up my lip
and in my best New England clip
with exact pronunciation
said *You are a nasty girl.*

Later, walking down
the street and eating pickled pigs' feet,
this southern delicacy that could
only be had
below the Mason-Dixon Line,
I thought about
immigrants and migration,
and why no one had warned me
to stay away from
fast fat girls in pink hot pants
who liked to defile young minds
and spoke an English that
was like a foreign language,
while trying to pick fruit
that didn't hang on a vine.

Fish Bait

It was unlikely that the bait grew
in these tubs
like specimens in a laboratory
watched over by a scientist in overalls
instead of a white lab coat.

It wasn't Latin that rolled off his tongue;
a Florida good old boy who knew his fish
and what could bring them
to the dinner table without a fuss.
A salesman able to hawk the most detestable
of wares:
worms and eels
and other things that went bump
in the night.

I dreaded this shop,
where light was forbidden,
the fetid contradiction of bathtubs full of dirt.
Here, I developed an allegiance with the Orthodox Jew
forbidden to eat the creeping and unclean
that moved along the ocean floor,
the law written upon my flesh
that crawled to be rid of this place.

Cleaning Fish

A fine art, not translatable to canvas
a spoon flaking scales, the paintbrush.
More doctor than artist really,
I watched my cousin slice
through a fish belly with the delicacy
of a surgeon, though his patient's gills had stopped
panting for life.

The fish filled the plate;
the whole so large it had to be fried in sections.
Nothing could take away from its beauty.
Not the baked beans
with a huge pat of butter slowly melting in their center.
Nor the kelly green-skinned cucumber slices
liberally graced with vinegar and black pepper,
or the sliced tomatoes with a smear of mayonnaise
passing for salad dressing.

Everyone savored the visual impact
like the memory of that one painting
when the gallery was left behind.
The fry grease long since placed
in its metal container,
only to be reopened
when the master returned
from another fishing trip,
new patients linked together
by their lower lips
and commenced to create again.

Bone and Socket
for Bennie White

She made eating chicken bones
look like a fine art.
Picture this,
a plate of wings fried
to perfection
and an ice cold Heineken
so chilly you had to wrap a
paper towel around it to handle.

As the conversation started getting heated,
those bones started snapping.
The soft, spongy bone tips nibbled
and chewed before the marrow
was sucked out like a milkshake through a straw.
The watching was more
educational than Mr. Smith's
high school physiology and anatomy
where everyone earned an A,
a consequence of his weak bladder
and our unwillingness to pass up
an opportunity to cheat.

This study of bones
had to be a byproduct of the Depression era
I reasoned, when people learned
not to waste anything like the marrow,
a second meal after the meat was gone.

I can still feel the pinch of my cousin's
grip on my arm as I went to throw
the smallest bone
of the chicken wing in the trash,
that grip that stopped me
mid-toss as she said
Uhh, uhh girl, give it here,
that's the best part.

Of Beer and Rattlesnakes on Sunday Morning

What was this strange Sunday ritual:
The women going to church on a cloud
of lily of the valley perfume,
while the men sat not so guiltily on the porch,
the telltale brown paper sack waiting on the ground.
They licked their lips in anticipation while speaking
that old lie, we'll be waiting until you get home
to tell us all about the sermon.

The snap and slither of that first can being opened
was a signal to start lying in earnest
about past women, fights won, and hard luck years
when neither the women nor the jobs were plentiful.

And that's when Peter Bo or Bo Pete that
lost sheep of the family who would mow
your lawn or wash your car for a pittance
came sauntering down the street with a rattlesnake
hanging dead from his hands.

He was delivering his Odyssean boast to anyone
who'd hear how a black man had slain the killer
before it slew him. So what if it was a shovel
instead of a shotgun that had won the day.

The men laughed and lobbed him a beer
because here in the flesh was the reason
why they shunned church on Sunday mornings,
the one day a workingman had to himself
to experience the contentment
of having to be nowhere at any specific time.

None of them would trade their lives
for anything else.
Being single would be a hardship
now that their flat stomachs had turned to paunch,
their full heads of nappy hair
now worn with a corona of baldness at the center.

They'd learned to accept their women, too.
Knew that they were no studs, but
a good wife never complained, just
closed her eyes and imagined
a good man who would one day share
her church pew and not notice how every now
and then she pulled a beer from his six-pack
just to remind herself of what holiness wasn't.

Post-Traumatic Race Disorder

A pickup backfires
and suddenly you are transported
from Knoxville, TN
six hours west
to Memphis.

It's Martin Luther King Day
in the bible belt
and you think
some native has gone nostalgic
and decided
you may not be him
but you're black enough
to pass.

You should have been able
to escape this duty,
but history follows you
like an old lover.
Boomerang.
Every year,
like clockwork,
you're volunteered
to commemorate your
lost leader's birth,
assuage white guilt.
For one more year
this is your moment,
the day they acknowledge you
so you can acknowledge him.
But someone forgot to tell you
how jumpy you'd get
on MLK Day
when a pickup backfires
and you think
this time
they've come for you.

Prayer Closet II

When Saul was on the road to Damascus
he was forced to answer to a new name and master.
I, too, somehow made to change
and wear bruises on bended knees.

They say it costs something to walk in an anointing,
to forgive the loving as well as deceitful
hands once laid upon your body,
like olive oil placed on your forehead
by saints and the not so saintly.

I have learned to draw out demons,
a work that is never done.
I tire, search for rest as my daughter peels
dead skin from my feet
revealing new, pink life beneath.
How can I answer her question,
*Mommy, how do you make the dead
stuff go away forever?*

I tell her not to believe people who tell you
you are only born once.
They know nothing
of going to sleep while you think you are living,
only to wake up one day and regret
the passing of years.
Somnambulance is just another word
for a heart in need of cleansing.

You must bow down I tell her,
bow down and let the refiner's hand
trouble the water.

A Gathering of Blooms
for Anastasia

I watch my child dart between swords of sunlight,
the day unwinding like an ordained path
beneath her feet.
Rebellion moves her out of reach of my voice
warning her away from house fronts,
strangers resurrecting their flowerbeds for spring,
and lawns still muddy from April showers.

Her partner in crime,
a sturdy bleached blond,
all of five years old
rushes to catch up and play male lead.
They decide to investigate a tulip bloom at the same time,
bump noses and part in laughter.
I smile in echo, thinking that ten years from now
they would not even be able to meet eyes
and shyly say hello.

I catch them whispering to each other about respective
boyfriends and girlfriends, knowing that to each other
they are simply friends.
Adults could learn a lot from these two.

I cannot pinpoint the exact moment when I realized
that I liked this job, mothering. Never a green thumb,
what had been given to me to grow, was.
I smelled lilac and my child's presence on a crisp breeze,
and it was good.

Saying Goodbye to the Dead

Moving makes me hum requiems
under my breath
watching you ponder anew
what to keep, what to mark
detritus.

The worse hoarders
prostitute junk
to casual bystanders,
pimp old coins, silver
with no maids to polish.

Your ancestors, Europeans,
called mine cannibals,
regardless of whether we partook
of the brain or heart,
somehow all pagans
lumped together
practiced the same art.
Yet I witness your informal altars
to the dead.
The worship of bits and pieces
of their lives
DNA and dust mingled forever.

Me, I like things new,
birthed from boxes
and bubble wrap.
Spiritless.
The scent of plastic
and leather
assembly-line fresh
like my love for you
new, without dust
and the baggage of history.